READERS

Flight from Bear Canyon

Anita Daher

ORCA BOOK PUBLISHERS

National Library of Canada Cataloguing in Publication Data

Daher, Anita, 1965-
Flight from Bear Canyon / Anita Daher.

(Orca young readers)
Sequel to: Flight from Big Tangle.
ISBN 1-55143-326-5

I. Title. II. Series.

PS8557.A35F538 2004   jC813'.6   C2004-904826-0

Library of Congress Control Number: 2004111203

Summary: In this sequel to *Flight from Big Tangle*, Kaylee must fly a plane for a second time, this time to rescue Jack, who has crashed his helicopter near a group of grizzlies.

Free teachers' guide available.

Orca Book Publishers gratefully acknowledges the support for its publishing programs provided by the following agencies: the Government of Canada through the Department of Canadian Heritage's Book Publishing Industry Development Program (BPIDP), the Canada Council for the Arts, and the British Columbia Arts Council.

Cover design by Lynn O'Rourke
Cover & interior illustrations by Stephen McCallum

In Canada:	In the United States:
Orca Book Publishers	Orca Book Publishers
1016 Balmoral Road	PO Box 468
Victoria, BC Canada	Custer, WA USA
V8T 1A8	98240-0468

07 06 05 04 • 6 5 4 3 2 1

Printed and bound in Canada
Printed on 100% post-consumer recycled paper,
100% old growth forest free, processed chlorine free
using vegetable, low VOC inks.

For Leslie, biter of life,
fountain of love and inspiration.
You're climbing new mountains now.
Go get 'em!

Acknowledgments

To begin, my heartfelt thanks to the Canada Council for the Arts and to First Air for making this trip possible. Thanks also to Rudy Klaus, fellow tourist and fine photographer, Mifi for putting me up and putting up with me in Yellowknife, and to the staff of Simpson Air—Ted, Terri, Charlene (also known as Mary) and Jean—who not only flew me into the park, but took complete care of me, providing food, friendship, a place to rest, and when I decided to stay an extra day, even arranged my travel back to Yellowknife through Air Tindi. People of Fort Simpson, you are golden.

1

Kaylee burped.

Other than the repeating taste of egg salad they'd had for lunch, the memory of her mother's hug was all she had to hold on to in this strange, wild place. Kaylee perched on the edge of a lake, staring at the northern mountain range her mother had disappeared beyond a short time earlier. The peaks were jagged, like broken teeth: a rocky wall keeping her from every-where she would rather be and everyone she would rather be with.

She was so engrossed in her gloomy study, she hadn't noticed she was no longer alone.

"Why are you here?"

Kaylee started, nearly slipping into the lake. She turned to see a girl roughly her age, head cocked to one side, short red curls framing a dirt-smudged face.

"I've been asking myself the same question," she answered, frowning.

Settling back onto her rock, Kaylee tucked a wayward strand of her long black hair behind her ear. She had been expecting this meeting. After all, the whole reason Mom had insisted on leaving her with Jack was so that Kaylee could hang out with his niece.

Mom had some stupid idea that Kaylee spent too much time alone. Kaylee argued that she wasn't alone—she had Sausage —but Mom said she needed someone who could offer better conversation than a basset hound. When the call came for Mom to help fight a big forest fire in Montana, she'd decided to leave Kaylee with Jack and his niece in the middle of these remote, sub-arctic mountains, never mind what Kaylee wanted.

The other girl's blue eyes locked onto Kaylee's green ones. She was a little shorter than Kaylee, but according to Mom would be going into grade six come fall just like her. She wondered if the other girl felt as pushed into this as she did.

"So, you're Jasmine?"

The girl gave an abrupt downward nod. "Jaz...no one calls me Jasmine."

Nearby, a deep bark sounded, followed by the snap-crackle of twigs as Sausage burst through the brush and barreled toward them, tongue lolling out the side of his mouth. Jaz extended a palm for Sausage to sniff. He ignored it and jumped up, knocking her backward into a patch of willow shrubs.

Kaylee covered a smile. "Jaz, meet Sausage."

"Ugh!" Jaz tried, and failed, to ward off his face washing. "Okay, nice Sausage—get off!"

Kaylee whistled the dog to her side, and Jaz pushed herself back upright.

"Sorry. He's not used to meeting new people."

The girl stared at her a moment, then broke into a slow, broad smile. The effect was stunning. It was like the sun high in the August sky was reflecting off of the lake, directly onto her face.

"I guess I'm not either." Jaz turned and motioned an arm over the lake. "Welcome, Kaylee," she said, spinning to include the mountains and boreal forest all around. "Welcome to my world. My world for the summer, anyway."

"Thanks...I guess."

Hidden Lake, home of Hidden Lake Lodge, was nestled between the Mackenzie Mountains of the Northwest Territories, and Logan Mountains of the Yukon. It was just a skip away from the mighty and mysterious South Nahanni River and Nahanni National Park Reserve. Mom had told Kaylee that prospectors used to call it the river of gold, not that they'd ever found much gold in it. She also said it was an ancient land, most of it untouched by the last ice age.

It might be old, but lots of people hadn't even heard of it. The few people who lived there had to travel pretty far to find a neighbor.

Until a wildfire destroyed their homes in Booker Bay a few months earlier, Jack had been their neighbor. He remained a close family friend. Like Mom—and Dad, before he died—Jack was a pilot, and often used his helicopter to help fight forest fires. Right now he was using it to help get his brother's new lodge ready for tourists, but since his brother was away at a tourism convention, Jack was fixing things up on his own.

"So…why are you here?" Jaz asked. "Uncle Jack told me about your mom fighting the fire. Don't you have any of your own family you could stay with?"

"Not in Canada," Kaylee said. She swallowed hard, dipping her fingers in the clear, cold water of the lake. She missed her Nana and Papa so much. She knew she would see them soon, though. Mom had promised they would fly to St. Lucia as soon as she finished with the fire down south.

A year ago, Kaylee's dad had disappeared while flying near St. Lucia. Ever since, Kaylee had felt as if her world had been turned inside out. After that terrible time, instead of spending the summer at Booker Bay and winter in St. Lucia, like they always had, Mom had made them move back to Booker Bay permanently, or at least until they got things "sorted out." Kaylee was just getting used to things again when the wildfire happened, and she had to summon all her courage to escape.

She had practically grown up in the backseat of an airplane, but she had never flown one until then. Her decision to fly her mother's floatplane over the burning brush could have been disastrous.

She glanced at the book she'd dropped casually beside her — *From the Ground Up*. After her unplanned flight, her mom was pretty shaken, and insisted she read about the theory of flight. Whatever. Other than the pictures it was pretty boring.

Jaz joined Kaylee on the sloping, lichen-covered boulder. Kaylee ignored her, watching Sausage as he ran along the curve of the lake. Her gaze wandered past the lodge to the far side, where two hippo-potamus-shaped hills of rock almost met, each dipping their snouts for a drink at the mouth of the river.

Kaylee could feel Jaz's constant stare and imagined the girl's green eyes burrowing into her skull like termites into wood. She scratched roughly at the phantom termites, and turned. "What...do I have a slug on my head or something?"

Again, the slow, broad smile. "No...I was just wondering if you want me to show you around."

"Maybe later, okay? My mom just left. I want to sit for a while."

"How long is she going to be gone?"

Kaylee shrugged. "Couple of weeks, maybe. After she gets back we'll be flying to St. Lucia to visit my Nana and Papa. We might even stay there." This wasn't exactly true, but it could happen. St. Lucia held many happy memories.

"What about school?"

"I'll probably home school. It's what I did before."

"On St. Lucia?"

"Uh-huh."

"Where's St. Lucia?"

"It's in the Caribbean."

"The Bermuda Triangle?"

Kaylee took a deep breath. She felt like she was being pelted by snowballs. "No…, it's south of that."

"Did your dad go missing in the Bermuda Triangle?"

Kaylee looked at her, mouth open. "No!" She got to her feet, brushing off small stones and dirt from her backside. "Look, no offense, but I don't want to talk right now, okay?"

Jaz shrugged. "Okay. It's just that lots of people disappear. Some turn up later. Sometimes way later."

Kaylee clenched her fists tight at her sides. "Look, he's not going to just…turn up. Okay?" Without waiting for a response, she snatched her book from the rock, and walked away, hoping her stay was closer to two days than two weeks.

Back at the lodge, she found Jack tinkering inside his brother's airplane. It was a Beaver. Compared to Mom's Cessna it looked chunky, and its nose was flat rather than pointed, as if a giant thumb had pushed it in.

"What's up, Kaylee?" Jack peered out the pilot's side door, pausing a moment before wiping his hands on a rag. "You look like you stepped in something unpleasant."

"I met Jaz." She sat on the edge of the dock, using the Beaver's closest pontoon as a footrest.

"Ah." Jack jumped from the pontoon to the dock, and dropped the wrench he'd been working with into a big red tool case. He began sliding things around, as if looking for something. "That's good. I'm sure Jaz appreciates your company."

"She has a funny way of showing it."

Jack gave up on whatever he'd been looking for, closed up his tool kit. "You have a fight already?"

She shrugged, scratching her nail against the rough wood of the dock.

"Tell you what," Jack said. "Hop in and we'll go for a spin. That might cheer you up."

Kaylee looked up, surprised. She hadn't seen him fly anything other than his helicopter as long as she'd known him. "You know how to fly this thing?"

"Of course!" he said, grinning. "You're not the only one who grew up around airplanes, you know. My pop used to fly for the Ontario Provincial Air Service. He flew this very Beaver, and when the Air Service decided to get rid of it, Pops bought it. This was the plane I learned to fly in — my brother too."

Kaylee settled into the right seat, running her fingers over the yoke. The Beaver was very different from Mom's Cessna. Unlike her mom's plane, it had matching controls on both sides of the cockpit. Instead of smooth leather-like vinyl on the walls and ceiling, it had a quilted, pinky-beige fabric that was coming away in places. Also, the rudder pedals were much farther away.

She crinkled her nose at the smell of oil mixed with something else … something sharp. Animal pelts, she thought, recognizing the same smell as in old Mr. Frank's trading counter in the general store back home.

It might not be pretty, and it smelled even worse, but Jack seemed to like it. He showed her how he used a wobble-pump to get it started, and they were airborne within seconds.

"Short take-off and landing," Jack explained, speaking through the mike on his headset. Kaylee was wearing a headset too — the engine noise would have been deafening without it. "We call it STOL for short. The Beaver is the best plane around for tight spaces. Anything it can get itself into, it can get itself out." Jack winked at her. "Better than we can say of most people."

As they circled back around the small lake, Kaylee noticed a slight, fiery-haired figure waving from shore. "Jack…did you tell Jaz about what happened?"

"You mean about the fire?"

"No. About my dad."

"It might have come up," he said, glancing at her. "Did she say something that made you feel bad?"

She frowned. "No…I don't know, maybe not on purpose. She sure asks a lot of questions."

11

Jack grinned. "She does, at that."

"Jaz said that sometimes when people go missing, they turn up."

"Ah. She might have been talking about Willy and Jake."

"Who?"

"Our resident ghosts." Jack chuckled as Kaylee looked up in alarm. "Don't worry, Kaylee. They're not the chain-clanking kind. More like an old mystery that was never completely sorted out. You ask Jaz about them. They're a hobby of hers."

Jack stopped talking as he lined up to land.

Well, Kaylee thought, her forced holiday at Hidden Lake Lodge might be interesting, after all.

2

Wisps of early morning mist rose from the lake like fingers stroking the air. Despite the dock being slick with dew, Kaylee sat and inhaled deeply. Same pine and lake-water smell as back home... but there was something else. Maybe it was because of the mountains.

She gasped as rays from the rising sun hit a bare jagged mountain range on the horizon. In the space of a sigh it changed in color from shadowed blue, to blazing gold, then red. Openmouthed, she watched as a large white bird with an impossibly long neck flew low over the mist, across the fire of the mountains.

"It's a trumpeter."

For the second time in as many days she jumped, nearly slipping into the lake. She frowned at the girl who had crept so silently into her morning. "What?"

"A trumpeter swan," Jaz explained, seating herself on the dock beside Kaylee. "I think there's a nesting pair somewhere near here. Haven't been able to find them, though."

"Another mystery."

Jaz looked at her, eyebrows raised.

"Jack said you'd tell me about Willy and Jake." Kaylee said.

Jaz grinned, and Kaylee again noticed how the day seemed to brighten around her. "Willy and Jake ... and the hidden treasure," she said, smirking.

Kaylee sat a little straighter. "Were Willy and Jake some kind of pirates?"

Jaz snorted. "You've spent too much time in the Caribbean." She stood and brushed herself off. "Where's your dog? Let's go for a hike, and I'll tell you about them."

Kaylee tilted her head, considering. If Jaz was at all bothered that they were being forced to spend time together, she didn't show it. She shrugged and stood, whistling. Instantly, a commotion erupted in the underbrush just beyond the narrow beach as Sausage bounded through horsetails and arctic cotton toward them. The mossy forest floor added hippity to his hop, making him look like a floppy-eared jackrabbit. Well, maybe if she squinted.

"Legend has it," Jaz began, leading the way up a worn trail, "that once upon a time in the summer of 1902, Willy Clifford was on his way to meet his brother Jake in the Yukon to stake a claim for a gold mine. He had to be careful, though, because he was on the run from a bunch of gambling debts he'd run up in California, and he was afraid someone would come after him."

Jaz moved quickly. Kaylee had to jog to keep up.

"He was seen entering the Nahanni River valley, but never came out the other end. After a while Jake went looking for him, and he never came out. Thing is, no one was waiting for Jake, so no one went looking for him."

"What happened?"

"Winter came, snow fell, and the next summer bones were discovered not far from here."

"Bones?" Kaylee gulped.

"Yup, poor Jake's. They knew they were his because of the claim papers they found. The bones were scattered—probably by bears or wolves —but they found the papers inside a pack in a lean-to he made from his boat. The boat had a hole in it. He must have hit a rock, and starved or froze to death waiting for someone to find him."

Kaylee shuddered. "So what happened to Willy?"

"A bunch of years later a guy named Bart Gunderson turned up at the Yellowknife hospital."

"So?"

"Turned out Bart was really Willy. He was pretty sick and decided to finally spill the beans. Said he hid and changed his name so the guys he was running from wouldn't track him down or get to his brother."

"Cool."

"It gets better." Jaz stopped at the top of a small crag overlooking Lost River, the feeder river that connected Hidden Lake to the South Nahanni River. She pointed suddenly. "Look!"

Kaylee spotted a flash of white over a stand of birch trees.

"Come on!" Jaz called, taking off into the brush after the disappearing swan.

A few minutes later they burst through shrubs peppered with tiny yellow flowers, onto a hard-packed clay trail. Sausage barked and ran ahead. Kaylee could hear the roar of what must be the South Nahanni.

Abruptly, Jaz stopped, and Kaylee tumbled into her. "Nuts!" Jaz cried.

"Sorry."

"No, not you," Jaz said, helping Kaylee to her feet. "The swan. I thought it might be nesting over here, but it must have flown to the other side of the South Nahanni."

"Can we cross?"

"No … the water is too fast."

Back at Lost River, Jaz lay back in a patch

of buttercups, plucking fat blueberries and popping them one by one into her mouth. Kaylee sat beside her, looking out over the gully, while Sausage sniffed the ground nearby.

"What's your favorite color, Kaylee?"

"Green, I guess."

"Mine too," Jaz said. "What's your favorite animal?"

"Can't you guess?"

"Bozo hounds?" she teased.

"Hey!" Kaylee cried, grasping a chunk of lace-like yellow caribou moss and lobbing it at the other girl. Jaz was okay, she thought. If she couldn't be with her mom, maybe hanging out at Hidden Lake Lodge wasn't so bad. It was her turn to ask a question. "Jaz, where do live when you're not here?"

Jaz pulled herself upright. "Yellowknife. My dad works for a tour company that brings people in to look at the northern lights, but we've been coming here to camp every summer for as long as I can remember. Dad's always wanted to run his own tourist lodge, and now he's gonna do it."

"Will you be going back to Yellowknife?"

Jaz cocked her head to one side, grinning. "Of course! This is still just for summers."

Kaylee thought about how similar their lives were, traveling from one home in summer to another in winter. "What happened to your mom?" she asked, fiddling with a bit of moss. Jaz shrugged. "She's in Edmonton. It's a two-day drive, but not so long by plane. Sometimes Dad flies me down to visit, and sometimes Mom comes to Yellowknife. They get along okay." She picked up a small handful of pebbles, and began throwing them into the gully, one by one.

Watching the water swirl and tumble over the rocks below made Kaylee think of poor Jake, who had set out in search of his brother and ended up waiting beside the river for someone to find him. "Jaz, you didn't finish Willy and Jake's story. You said there was treasure. Jake only left bones and papers. Did Willy strike it rich?" Jaz laughed abruptly. "You win the cookie!"

At the word "cookie," Sausage sat straight, looking expectantly at Jaz. Kaylee pulled a biscuit from her pocket and tossed it to him, noting with pride how easily he jumped and plucked it from the air.

"Everyone figured Willy had gone crazy. Said he found paradise, but wouldn't say where it was. Said he lived alone in his paradise for ten years before settling a couple of hundred miles downstream in the town of Nahanni Butte. Said he got married there and discovered what paradise truly was." Jaz rolled her eyes. "When they told him how his brother died looking for him, he put one hand over his eyes and the other over his heart, and said, 'My secret ain't worth nuthin' now.' Then he croaked. That's the story I heard, anyhow."

"And you think the secret is treasure?"

"Sure. Most people think he found Nahanni gold. Some say the gold is cursed. Others say he took it as he needed it and didn't want anyone else to touch it. Either way, he wouldn't say where it was."

"Some story. So where do you think it is?"

Jaz shrugged. "Wherever it is, I'll bet there's a clue in that paradise of his. But all the cabins along the river have been pretty well explored. Maybe he lived in a cave — there are hundreds of them around here." She grinned. "Maybe some day I'll show you my own secret hideout."

Hidden treasure — secret hideouts. Jaz was just as loaded with mystery as this strange land.

Kaylee looked beyond the river gully to distant mountains, silver in the morning sun. Somewhere before those mountains, amid moss-covered hills, tree-stubbled peaks and the great bare canyons lining the winding South Nahanni River, a mystery lay, long buried but never laid to rest.

Somewhere lay Willy's paradise, and Jake's end.

3

"Tell me again how you flew your mom's plane," Jaz said, leaning against the doorframe of Kaylee's room.

Kaylee was stretched out on her bottom bunk, flipping through *From the Ground Up* while Sausage slept on a mat on the floor. The soft tapping of rain against the window had made her dozy. She stretched and reached down to scratch her hound's speckled belly. "Oh, come on Jaz. It wasn't that big a deal."

"You're kidding, right?"

"No..." She swung her legs over the edge of the bed. "Okay, maybe it was a big deal... it was really scary. It's just that

I've been in airplanes since I was a baby. I watched my mom and dad take off and land a million times."

"I've flown with my dad lots too. Watching is different from doing."

Kaylee grinned. "That's just what my mom said."

Jaz nodded toward the flight manual. "If you already know how to do it, why are you reading about it?"

Kaylee tossed the book aside. "It makes my mom feel better. Don't know why … I'm not likely to ever get stuck in a forest fire again." She swallowed. "Not if I can help it, anyway."

"No forest fires around here," Jaz said, nodding her chin toward the window. It had been pouring cats and dogs for three days.

Kaylee frowned. "The lake is getting pretty high. If it keeps raining, Jack is going to have to move his helicopter farther up the beach."

Jaz was peering out the window. "I think our luck is about to change."

Just like that the cloud cover broke apart and sunshine flooded the room.

"Come on!" Jaz called, bounding out the door. "Let's go hiking!"

Sausage barked, following.

Kaylee was surprised at how much she'd been enjoying Jaz's company. Ordinarily, she would have gone stir crazy cooped up inside for so long, but it had actually been fun. Jaz had told her about ancient queens and headless gold hunters, all legends of the Nahanni, and, in turn, she'd taught Jaz how to say the phonetic alphabet —the one pilots use when they talk on their radios.

"See you later, Uncle Jack!"

Jack was sitting in the small office, listening to the bush radio. About this time every morning the operator broadcast the weather forecast. "Where are you going?" he called.

"Crazy," Jaz answered, pulling on her boots. "Unless we get out hiking right now!"

Jack chuckled. "Okay…fine," he said, "but don't go far until we know that the weather is going to stay good. You know how fierce sudden rain can be around here."

They didn't need a forecast to tell them that the day had taken a turn for the better. The gray cloud that had hugged the hills for days was breaking up and lifting, revealing a brilliant blue sky. The sudden sun was so warm that steam rose from the Beaver, which was moored to the not-quite-flooded dock. It was August in the Northwest Territories. Nights were cool, but summer wasn't finished yet.

Kaylee whistled, and Sausage bounded back from the trail ahead of them. His feet and the bottoms of his ears were covered in mud. Jaz stopped at a fork in the path, studying a shrub laden with heavy orange berries.

"What's up?" Kaylee asked. "Don't you know where you're going?"

"Of course I do, flygirl. I was just wondering if I should show you my hideout."

"Yes-yes-yes!"

Jaz grinned, eyes twinkling. "Do you think you're worthy?"

Kaylee dropped to one knee and clasped her hands in front of her. "Oh please, Lady Jaz, queen of this great wild wilderness, will you show me your hidden castle?"

"Yankee-Echo-Sierra!" Jaz answered, giggling, spelling out "yes" in the phonetic alphabet. "Even if you are a mud-covered peasant."

Kaylee stood straight, laughing, rubbing at the fresh mud she'd just ground into her jeans. Following Jaz up the right fork, Kaylee decided that she was the most interesting kid she'd ever met.

They chatted happily as they hiked around Hidden Lake to follow the far side of Lost River toward the South Nahanni. Before long they were climbing steadily. "I would have taken you here before, but rain makes the trail too slippery," Jaz said, puffing slightly. "It's mostly clay along the climbing part."

The path narrowed, slicing between two walls of stone, still rising. Finally, they arrived at the top.

"Whoa…" Kaylee breathed.

The view was stunning. They were about a half-mile up from the South Nahanni River, its dark water snaking between canyon walls below. The rock walls lining the river were sheer, with horizontal lines running through, making each surface look like a whacko layer cake with about a hundred layers. In places it looked like someone had piled blocks, one on top of another.

Jaz pointed south. "Virginia Falls and the park are that way," she said. "This is Bear Canyon, and up that way," she said, pointing north, "is where they found Jake's bones."

"Is it like this all along the river?" Kaylee asked, still wide-eyed.

"No. Sometimes the cliffs cut straight up from the river, like here in the canyon, but in other places the mountains are set back a ways. If you sit quiet you see lots of animals—Dall's sheep and caribou mostly. Once I saw a grizzly bear."

"Were you scared?"

"Nah. It was on the other side of the river, and the current was too fast for it to cross."

She ran her fingers gently along the rock wall behind them, touching tube-like outcrops stacked one on top of another. "This looks like coral," she mused.

Jaz shrugged. "It probably is."

"It can't be! Coral is only in the ocean."

"This was an ocean, silly," Jaz said, as if everyone was supposed to know it, "about a million years ago."

"You said there are caves. Where are they?"

Jaz grinned and nodded toward the canyon walls. "Look."

Kaylee frowned and studied the rock surface more carefully. "I see dark spots. Are those all caves?"

"Some. Like I said, there are hundreds of caves around here. Most are off-limits to tourists."

"Show me yours!"

"Did I say my hideout was a cave?"

"I guessed."

"You're one smart cookie, Kaylee."

At the word "cookie," Sausage gave Jaz his full attention and barked. Kaylee laughed and tossed him a biscuit. "Maybe you should watch what you say around Sausage...I'm almost out of biscuits."

At the word "biscuit," Sausage barked again, and both girls laughed.

"Say," Jaz began, "that Sausage is one smart..."

"Don't say it!"

"Okay, okay." Jaz was giggling now. She hooked her arm in Kaylee's and began walking up the path once more. "You're pretty cool, Kaylee."

Kaylee grinned. "So are you, Jaz."

"It's almost like we're sisters."

"It's weird how much alike our lives are," Kaylee said, nodding. "We both have parents who are pilots...we live in one place in the summer and another in the winter."

"Maybe one day we really will be family," Jaz said, glancing sideways at Kaylee.

"What do you mean?"

Jaz stopped. "What if Uncle Jack and your mom are more than just friends?"

Kaylee felt alarm, white hot and sudden. Her heart beat faster. She swallowed and spoke slowly. "My mom and Jack are just friends, Jaz. They've been friends for a long time."

Jaz didn't seem to notice Kaylee's discomfort. "Sure, 'just friends' now, but maybe they'll get romantic someday."

Kaylee stepped back from Jaz, shaking her head. "How can you say that?"

"Easy!" Jaz continued. "You already told me they like each other lots. If they get married, we'll be cousins!"

Kaylee couldn't bear to hear another word. Tears sprang to her eyes. "Take it back Jaz…take it back!" she said, her voice rising.

"What do you mean?"

"My mom loves my dad."

"But your dad died…"

"I can't believe you would say that!" Kaylee was shouting now. "Just because your mom and dad don't love each other…"

"What?" Jaz looked hurt now.

"My mom won't ever love anyone else. Too bad you don't know what that's like!"

Jaz opened her mouth wide in shock.

Without saying another word, she gave Kaylee a hard shove. As Kaylee tumbled to the ground, Jaz turned and ran on up the path, out of sight.

Sausage began to follow, but Kaylee whistled him back. She wiped her wet cheeks in the ruff of his neck and hugged him close.

"Stupid Jaz," she whispered. "Sausage, you will always be my best and only friend."

4

Back at the lodge, Jack was preparing his helicopter for flight. "Kaylee!" he called, as she walked toward his makeshift beach landing pad. "I'm glad you're back." He looked ready to burst with excitement.

"What's going on, Jack?"

"Just got a call from the park ranger. A pilot reported a large gathering of grizzly bears at the mouth of Bear Canyon."

"I thought grizzly bears traveled alone."

"Usually," he said, setting a rather large camera inside. "The mouth of Bear Canyon flooded, and several caribou drowned trying to cross. The bears are having a feeding frenzy. I want to take pictures before it starts raining again."

Kaylee's stomach churned at the thought of those poor caribou.

"Go get Jaz, Kaylee. She'll want to see this too."

She hesitated. Should she tell Jack that Jaz wasn't here? She didn't want to mention their fight. If she did, Jack might ask what they fought about.

"Um … okay. I think she's in her room," she said and jogged up the boardwalk toward the lodge, Sausage at her heels.

She waited a few minutes inside and jogged back out to the helipad. "She's tired, Jack. She wants to stay here."

Jack frowned. "That's too bad. Well … I suppose she's seen them before. Hop in, Kaylee, we'll bring her back pictures."

"I'm kind of tired too, Jack. I'll wait here … okay?"

"What? You have to come, Kaylee. I need you to take pictures. Besides, we're not likely to get another chance like this. Back in Booker Bay, we don't get grizzly bears at all."

She hesitated. Maybe it wouldn't be so bad…as long as she didn't have to look at any dead caribou. Besides, if it meant avoiding Jaz for a little while longer she was all for it. "Okay, Jack. I guess."

"Good girl!" he said. "Get in. Looks like Sausage is coming too."

Sausage had already jumped in through the open door and made himself comfortable on the floor.

Flying between the canyon walls was amazing; sheer gray rock splashed with red and yellow, rising to what seemed like forever left her breathless and feeling very small. At the mouth of Bear Canyon, however, the carnage was awful—much worse than Kaylee had imagined. The glass bubble of the cockpit brought the world to her feet, the ten or twelve grizzly bears with their bloody paws and muzzles and torn bodies of caribou, almost in her lap.

"Take a picture, Kaylee!"

"I can't, Jack," she said weakly. "I think I'm going to be sick."

Jack studied her face, his brow creased. "Okay...we'll fly up the river a bit, turn around and give it another go. If you don't feel up to taking pictures, you can hold the controls for me while I take a few shots."

Beyond the mouth of Bear Canyon, the river widened, with sloping mountains and some flooding of flatlands at its edge. Kaylee strained to find pathways. Somewhere in there Jaz might still be hiding out, angry, even though she was the one who'd been wrong.

"Feeling better?" asked Jack.

She nodded. "A bit."

"Okay. We'll turn around."

He swung out over a wide, flat area. Bunches of purple fireweed edged a stand of soft green tamarack, their needles just beginning to turn yellow. An overflow of water spread out just beyond.

"Does the river flood often, Jack?"

"Every time we get a good..."

BANG!

The view through the cockpit bubble shifted wildly sideways.

Kaylee braced one hand against the glass, the other on the control panel. "Jack...what's wrong?"

He was silent, concentrating on the controls. The helicopter leveled out after a moment, but began swinging around from front to back, each swing faster than the last.

"Jack!"

"Hang tight, Kaylee—crash position. It's my tail rotor...must have lost the drive belt."

Kaylee leaned forward, clasping her hands above her head, as the world outside the bubble swung back and forth. Her heart was beating so fast she thought she might forget to breathe. The helicopter rotated wildly. For the second time since leaving the lodge Kaylee thought she might be sick.

"It's okay, Kaylee...we're almost down."

Suddenly there was another loud bang. Kaylee opened her eyes just in time to see the woods rushing toward them.

5

Kaylee shut her eyes tight, afraid of what she might see. She wiggled her fingers and toes and tried to straighten her legs. Her knee hurt a little, but she thought she was okay.

A warm tongue washed her cheeks—Sausage! She wrapped her arms around her dog and opened her eyes. The glass of the cockpit had been pierced by something, maybe a tree branch. The glass hadn't shattered, but it had turned white from thousands of tiny crack lines. It was pushed in, though not all the way. The helicopter looked ruined.

"Jack?" she whispered.

He was slumped against his seat. Eyes closed. Sausage sniffed at him and whined.

"Jack?" Kaylee called again, her stomach twisting.

He groaned and opened his eyes. "Kaylee...are you okay?" He tried to sit up and cried out.

"Jack...what's wrong?"

"I think my leg is broken."

Kaylee gave her head a shake. She didn't understand. A moment ago they were flying along the river. There had been a loud noise. "We crashed, Jack," she said softly. She'd been flying all her life...she'd never been in a crash.

"I'm so sorry, honey," Jack said. Grunting, he flipped the radio switch and spoke into his headset mike. "Any aircraft, any aircraft, Mayday, Mayday, Mayday."

The words brought tears to Kaylee's eyes, panic to the surface. They had crashed in the Northwest Territories. Really crashed.

She held her breath, listening for a response. Nothing.

"Jack...what if no one hears?"

He spoke again into his headset mike. "Any aircraft, any aircraft...we've crashed just north of Bear Canyon along the South Nahanni...Mayday, Mayday, Mayday."

They waited. Nothing. Jack sighed, his forehead creased deeply. "Don't worry Kaylee. Jaz will hear the radio and call for help."

Kaylee gulped. "What if she doesn't, Jack?"

"The helicopter's emergency beacon will have kicked off on impact. A satellite will pick up the alarm and alert search and rescue crews."

"I don't hear anything."

Jack closed his eyes, his pain clear. "You won't. The alarm is sent by radio signal on the emergency channel. I usually keep my backup radio tuned to that frequency, but it's been on the fritz. I was trying to fix it just before we left."

She looked behind her. In her mom's plane, the bright orange emergency locator box was attached behind the back row of passenger seats. All she could see in the crumpled, twisted cab of Jack's helicopter were maps strewn where they shouldn't be, and the camera. She twisted her head to look underneath the panel. It was caved in underneath. She swallowed.

"It's outside, attached to the tail boom," Jack said, reading her mind.

"What if it's not working?"

Jack reached for the channel selector on his radio, and flipped it to 121.5—the emergency channel. After a moment, he tapped at it, frowning. "We should be hearing the alarm now. Either the beacon is broken, or the radio is."

Jack turned the mike on again, and repeated his mayday call.

The reality of what had happened—was still happening—hit Kaylee like a whump in the belly. "Jack...we can't just sit here. We've got to do something!"

"Don't worry, Kaylee."

"How can you say that, Jack? It's obvious that *you're* worried!" Her voice was rising.

"Calm down!" Jack snapped.

Kaylee froze, openmouthed. Sausage cocked his head.

Jack ran his hand through his hair. "Kaylee, this situation isn't great, but we need to stay calm. I'd say we were incredibly lucky. In all likelihood, the emergency beacon is working just fine. Even if this radio is broken, the one back at the house won't be. Jaz will hear the emergency signal and call for help on the satellite phone."

Kaylee hung her head and began to cry. Jack reached over awkwardly and tucked a strand of hair behind her ear. "I mean it honey. Don't worry."

"It's not that, Jack," she sniffled. "It's just…"

"What is it?"

She took a deep breath. "Jaz isn't at the lodge, Jack. I don't know where she is."

Jack was looking steadily at her, as if trying to unlock the puzzle in what she had just said. She stared at her knees, then at what was left of the window—anywhere but Jack's eyes. "She wasn't with me when I came back to the lodge. We had a fight, and she took off. I think she went to her hideout."

At first, Jack said nothing. Kaylee peeked at him as he rubbed his hand over his eyes. "I see," he said, finally.

"Will someone still hear the beacon?" she asked in a small voice.

"I hope so."

"Jaz will go home eventually. She has to. She'll call for help then."

"I'm sure you're right, Kaylee."

It was a sensible thought, but it didn't ring true. Jaz would have no idea where they had gone. She might call for help when they didn't show...but what good would that do? Nobody knew they'd gone to see the bears. The park ranger might guess, but what if no one called him? They'd just have to sit tight and hope.

Kaylee shivered, thinking about poor Jake who had died waiting — maybe not far from where they had crashed.

A thought occurred to her and she turned to Jack, "What about the bears?"

"What about them?"

Kaylee stood just a little, peering out a hole in the crackled glass. The helicopter had come to rest pointing downriver, but the mouth of the canyon was too far away to see. "What if they come upriver and find us?"

Jack tried to reach behind his seat, but cried out in pain. "Kaylee, get behind here and pull out the bag. It's my survival kit."

She did as she was asked, pulling the red canvas bag to the front. Jack rummaged through, finally pulling out a flare gun and four cartridges. "It's not much, but it'll do in a pinch."

"Will that stop a grizzly bear?"

"Let's hope."

Jack laid his head back and closed his eyes. His skin had taken on a grayish pallor that Kaylee didn't like.

Setting her shoulder against the left side passenger door, she gave it a push. It opened easily. Most of the damage was to the front and Jack's side of the helicopter, as well as the rotor blades on top. When Jack had tried to set it down, the swinging tail boom must have thrown them toward the trees. Stepping away, she shook her head. Jack was right—they'd been lucky.

It was so quiet. All she could hear was the river washing past and an odd sound of shifting stones. An eagle called from somewhere deep in the mountains. For the first time Kaylee had a sense of how very alone they were. Other than Jaz, wherever she was, the closest person would be a few hundred miles downriver in Nahanni Butte, the town where Willy had settled. What if it took a long time for someone to find them?

She walked around the curve of the newly flooded lake and looked back downriver. About two soccer-field lengths away, the river curved eastward toward the canyon. If a grizzly bear came upriver, they wouldn't see it until it was almost upon them.

She kicked at the dirt.

"Jack!" she called, jogging back. "Jack, I'm going for help!"

6

Jack rubbed his eyes. "What do you mean?" He looked and sounded groggy.

Kaylee leaned in through the open door. "We can't sit here waiting for a bear to decide we smell like caribou. If the emergency beacon isn't going off, it could be ages before anyone comes to find us." She dropped her head. "Besides, it's my fault Jaz doesn't know where we are."

When she looked up, she saw that Jack had closed his eyes again. After a minute he opened them, pulled a pen out of his pocket and picked up one of the maps. "Okay, Kaylee." He nodded his head slowly. "Anyone else I wouldn't let go alone, but you've always had good outdoors sense. Besides, we're actually not that far from home." He spread the map out on the seat beside him. "Here's the lodge...and we're here."

Using the pen, he made big dots to show each place. According to the map, the South Nahanni River actually bent like an elbow. Hidden Lake was off the top of one arm, and their crash site near the top of the other. If she walked straight the distance would be only one-quarter of what it would be if she walked along the river canyon.

Through the open door Jack pointed to the sloping mountain she would have to climb. "That's Blood Peak. Once you climb up a ways, you'll see where you can cut between it and a smaller peak that goes toward the canyon. Once you're close to the lodge you won't need the compass — Sausage will be sniffing for his dinner."

He reached back into the survival kit and pulled out a compass and a whistle. "Here," he said. "Same safety rules apply here as anywhere. Animals don't like to be surprised—especially bears. Make some noise as you walk and toot the whistle every now and then. Any animals in your path will likely try to avoid you."

"Thanks, Jack," she said, her stomach fluttering. She pocketed the whistle and checked the compass. According to the map, the lodge was to the southwest.

"You'll be fine," Jack said softly.

"I know." She clamped her jaw, and stood straight.

"One more thing..."

"What?"

"This mess isn't your fault, Kaylee."

She stared at her toes.

"Whether or not you told Jaz is beside the point," he said gravely. "I should have told the park ranger that we were coming out here and what time to expect us back." He shook his head. "Any good pilot knows that."

She swallowed. "I'll try the radio when I get back to the lodge, and I'll call for help on the satellite phone."

"Good girl," Jack said. He smiled, then winced in pain. "You'd better get moving."

She took a deep breath, gave Jack a mock salute and closed the door to the helicopter.

Sausage had his nose buried in a patch of mountain avens, their delicate white faces wide open as if smiling toward the sun. A shadow passed over as a lone gray cloud scuttled like a spider across the blue.

She whistled sharply. "Come on, Sausage. Let's go home, boy." She glanced one more time downriver, and set off toward Blood Peak, Sausage bounding eagerly ahead.

The ground near the river had been mostly sand and pebbly stone, but as she began climbing up slope, it quickly turned to a mix of clay and rich brown earth— almost black. Ahead, the trees crowded close together, shoulder to shoulder. She checked her compass and chose her path.

Despite the weight of her task, she was awed by the beauty surrounding her. Lodgepole pine stood straight and slim like telephone poles or some sort of wild guardians with short stubby arms. Ferns fanned the ground at their feet like feathery skirts brushing a carpet of moss, spongy green and laced with yellow. As she climbed she glanced at farther off mountain peaks. Some were smaller, capped with green and brown. Others were topped with snow and ice, or partly hidden in cloud. The sky was peppered with mashed-potato clouds, their bases flat and gray.

Her climb eased at a broad plateau. She strode into a tangle of knee-high grass and wildflowers, pushing through deep blue trumpets of larkspur. The hum of insects grew louder. "Mosquitoes," she muttered, waving her hand in front of her face. There were lots more than there were five minutes ago. Maybe she was close to a swampy area.

In answer the spongy moss got spongier, and her boots sucked against mud.

"Man, this is bad!" she exclaimed, slapping at her neck. Sausage was bounding ahead like a deer over a ditch and didn't seem bothered. She tried leaping in the same manner, but it didn't help, and she was soon short of breath. At least she was through the wet patch.

The air tickled her nose with scents of sweet flower blossoms and tangy pine, but she couldn't fill her lungs with enough. She took a deeper breath and swallowed a mosquito. "Blagggh!" She coughed and tried to bat away bugs as she jogged.

Abruptly, her path came to an end at a bald outcrop of rock as tall as a garden shed. She would have to veer off her compass heading until she could find a pathway around it. But which way should she go? She slapped at her head and scratched fresh bites, studying the rock. Dark green plants with leaves that reminded her of frost on glass grew in the cracks. She pulled on a clump—it came out easily. If she could pull out enough weeds, she could step in the cracks left behind, and climb the rock face. Sausage wouldn't be able to go up that way, but at least she could have a look around and try to figure out the best way to get back on track.

"Ow!" She scratched at a fresh bite beside her nose, noting a pleasant lemony smell on her hands—just like the citronella grass her mom used to grow in her garden back home. Mom would crush it and use the oil to keep mosquitoes at bay, rather than covering herself in chemicals. Should she try doing the same? She frowned. It might smell like citronella, but it sure didn't look anything like it. What if it was something bad and it gave her a rash?

As another mosquito bit between her shoulder blades, she decided it was worth the risk. She pulled out clump after clump, crushing the leaves with her hands, and rubbing the oil first on her hair and exposed skin, then on her clothes.

She waited. No rash so far ... and the mosquitoes seemed to be giving her a break. Even if it didn't last long, it was a relief. She whistled for Sausage and rubbed the oil all over him. As Kaylee massaged his coat, his tongue lolled out the side of his mouth. To him this was all good fun—a nice petting.

Putting one foot in a crack and gripping an outcrop with her hand, she began pulling herself up. Setting her cheek flat against the cool grit of stone, she reached for another step, and another. With a grunt, she pulled herself over the top.

Sausage whined loudly. Looking down, she saw him sitting, staring up at her. "Just a minute, boy!"

She stood and looked about. To one side, the steep rock face stretched higher up the mountain, finally vanishing into a blanket of low cloud that now almost blacked out the sun. She looked the other way. It was hard to tell for sure, but it looked like that way the rock dipped, getting smaller, finally disappearing into a snarl of weeds and underbrush.

"That probably means more mosquitoes," she muttered. Should she chance it and climb higher up the mountain? She could always come back if she didn't find a way around. No, she decided, there's no time—she had to get help for Jack. She'd just have to brave the bugs and trust in the crushed plant.

She half climbed, half slid back down the rock surface and began jogging down her chosen path, Sausage at her heels.

Pushing aside tangled branches and tall grass for Sausage was tedious, but slowly she made her way through to more open ground. Thankfully, the mosquitoes thinned out with the weeds. It was just as Jack promised. She could see where Blood Peak joined with another that rose toward Bear Canyon. She checked the compass again and picked up her pace.

Sausage suddenly *gruffed* and ran ahead. Kaylee stopped and stared, mouth open. The earth was a mix of sand and clay. In it she could clearly see the broad print of a bear claw. From its size, she guessed it was a grizzly.

She couldn't breathe. Should she blow her whistle?

To her left she heard rustling. With another *gruff,* Sausage bounded back toward her and jumped past her into the woods.

Something was crashing through the underbrush, coming her way!

7

"Down, boy!" Jaz cried, jumping onto the path.

Kaylee exhaled sharply. "Jaz! I thought you were a bear."

Jaz didn't smile. Neither did Kaylee. Jaz kicked at the dirt between them before speaking. "I saw you from my hideout. What are you doing out here?"

"It's Jack," Kaylee said, swallowing. "We've got to get back to the lodge." As Kaylee quickly explained what happened, Jaz stared at her, mouth open.

The heavens chose that moment to open, and a torrent of rain cascaded down, pelting Kaylee's skin so hard she was sure it would leave bruises.

"I doubt this will last," Jaz shouted. "Follow me."

Under the canopy of tightly packed trees, they were sheltered from direct impact, though still soaked through in seconds. They pushed through until they reached a small clearing. Jaz dashed toward a rock face on the other side and climbed a short, narrow path to a cave opening, beckoning Kaylee to follow.

Out of the rain, Kaylee looked about her, stunned. "This is so cool!" she breathed.

The cave was about twice Kaylee's height, with the space of a kitchen. Stalactites hung down. Stalagmites pointed up. In some places the rock was whitish, and in others it was orange, yellow and green. To one side of the cave opening, the rock looked like porridge spilled from a pot. Everywhere, it was damp.

Jaz looked at her shyly. "At first I was going to leave you, but..." She shrugged. "I thought you might be lost."

Kaylee swallowed. "I'm sorry I said those things about your mom and dad, Jaz. I was just mad."

Jaz studied her a moment, then gave one of her abrupt downward nods. "It's okay." She looked at her feet. "I'm sorry I said those things about your mom and Uncle Jack. I didn't mean to make you mad, or hurt your feelings or whatever."

"I know."

Both girls stood in silence. There didn't seem to be much else to say. Even though they had both apologized, Kaylee didn't feel as close to the other girl as she had that morning. She tucked the compass in her pocket and peered out at the driving rain. "You said it wouldn't last long. How do you know?"

"Just a guess. It's coming down too hard to be steady rain like before, and showers never last long."

"I've never been in a cave," Kaylee said.

"Even if you had, it wouldn't have been as nice as mine," Jaz said, motioning Kaylee toward a corner set up with wooden crates and blankets.

"I piled moss underneath this blanket so I've got a place to sit." Jaz said, moving a rock from the top of a small crate and lifting its lid. "Inside here I've got snacks." She tossed Kaylee a bag of chips, then opened the other crate. "And inside here I keep books and stuff."

Inside the second crate Kaylee spotted a stack of comics and chapter books, a flashlight and a dirt-smudged deck of cards. "Nice," she said.

Jaz offered a slight smile, and Kaylee grinned back. Maybe they could be friends again after all.

Kaylee moved back to the cave opening and looked into the clearing. It was still pouring, but she could see where Jaz would have seen her coming from Blood Peak. The cave made a perfect lookout. "Are we far from the lodge?" she asked.

"No. Just around the corner and down the mountain. It's about a twenty-minute hike."

She hugged herself. "It's cold in here."

Jaz handed her one of the blankets,

and she wrapped it around her shoulders. Poor Jack, she thought. The rain would be getting into the helicopter through the ruined windshield. He'd be wet and cold, and he didn't have a blanket.

"Come on," Jaz said. "We might as well have a snack."

Sausage sat up straight on the make-shift carpet as Jaz unwrapped a granola bar. She broke off a piece and tossed it to him. Kaylee opened her bag of chips, but found she wasn't hungry after all. She rolled the top closed and set it on the blanket beside her.

"Uncle Jack will be okay," Jaz said, reading her mind. "He's camped out plenty of times. A little rain won't bother him. Besides, it already sounds like it's letting up." She tucked the empty granola wrapper in her pocket.

"I'm more worried about grizzly bears," Kaylee said, biting her lip.

Sausage growled softly.

Jaz snorted. "It's like he's agreeing with you."

Both girls fell silent as Sausage stood, hackles raised, and walked stiff-legged toward the opening of the cave.

"I think something is out there," Kaylee whispered.

The only sound coming from outside was that of the wind and rain. Inside, Sausage's soft and steady growl mingled with the sound of water trickling through twists and openings in the limestone of the cave.

Shrugging the blanket from her shoulders, Kaylee stepped quickly to the opening. What she saw made her blood run cold. Wide-eyed, she turned to Jaz and mouthed the word, "bear."

In the clearing, a honey-colored grizzly bear was slowly swinging its great head from side to side, sniffing. It had a white patch on its left shoulder, as if someone had taken white paint and splashed it against one side of the hump on its back. It wasn't huge, by grizzly standards, but it was still terrifying.

Jaz joined her at the opening, glanced outside and flattened herself against the inside wall.

Kaylee tried to remember her bear safety rules. Noise. If the bear was just being curious, they might be able to scare it away with a little noise. She pulled out her whistle. "We need something to bang," she whispered to Jaz.

Jaz nodded, grabbed the lid from one of the crates, and the rock that had held it down. Kaylee put the whistle in her mouth.

"Ready?" Jaz whispered.

Kaylee nodded, but held her hand up, motioning for Jaz to wait a moment. She peeked back outside. The bear was about twenty feet away, standing tall on its hind legs, still sniffing the air. The rain didn't seem to bother it. Sausage's growl reached a fevered pitch, and he launched himself out the door.

"Sausage!" Kaylee cried.

8

Sausage scrambled down the narrow path, and faced the bear, growling and snarling.

"Sausage!" Kaylee wailed. "Sausage! Come back, boy!" She snatched Jaz's rock from her hands and launched it toward the bear.

Jaz pulled her back. "Are you crazy?" she cried.

Kaylee turned back to the clearing, nerves on fire. She tried whistling. "Here, boy! Come on back, Sausage!"

The dog ignored her.

"If Sausage jumps at him," Jaz said, "he'll make the bear mad. It might even come after us."

"What can we do?" Kaylee blinked through gathering tears, watching the terrible ballet play out below. Sausage circled, growling, and the bear stood its ground, bellowing back.

"We've got to get out of here," Jaz whispered.

"No!" she cried. She couldn't leave without Sausage. He was only trying to protect her. It hurt to swallow. "Besides, unless you've got a back door we're stuck."

Jaz frowned and pulled her flashlight out of the crate. "Maybe I do." She pointed the light toward a dark corner, showing an opening not much bigger than a cupboard.

"A tunnel?"

"I'm not sure."

"Haven't you checked it out?"

"Just the opening…I never had a reason to go farther. Even if it doesn't go anywhere, it's a place to hide. The bear can get into the cave, but it would never fit in there." She bit her lip. "I hope not, anyway."

Kaylee looked back at Sausage and whistled again, knowing it wouldn't make a difference. It didn't. Sausage growled and snapped, and the bear was beginning to snarl back, slapping at the hound with one of its great paws.

"I can't leave him," she said, tears sliding down her cheeks.

"Come on, Kaylee," Jaz said. "We're only making things worse by being here."

She knew Jaz was right. If she stayed in the cave, Sausage would continue to try and protect them. If she were out of sight, there was a chance he might run away.

"Okay," she said weakly. Her stomach flipped — she felt she might throw up.

Reluctantly, she followed Jaz, crawling on hands and knees through the opening. She could hear water trickling all around as it pooled against her knees.

Jaz cast the light on slightly higher ground. "Come on," she said.

They pulled themselves out of the wet onto a beach of loose stone, hunching forward to fit under the sloping ceiling. It was like some strange black shore on another planet. Jaz continued to poke the light into dark corners.

Kaylee strained to hear past water, trickling, pattering and dripping, tinkling like a xylophone. Nothing. At least she hadn't heard Sausage cry out.

This new part of the cave was spooky, nothing like Jaz's hideout.

A crash sounded nearby, and the girls looked at each other in alarm. Could it be the bear? Was it in Jaz's cave?

They listened as the crash was followed by heavy snuffling, a crinkling sound and chewing.

"My chips," Kaylee mouthed at Jaz, who nodded. It had to be the bear. Kaylee knew Sausage's sniffing and eating sounds, and this wasn't him.

Sausage got away, she thought with relief. He'd likely follow the scent of Jaz's earlier footprints and find his way back to the lodge. After all, basset hounds had the second best sniffers in all the dog family. Bloodhounds had the best.

A grunt echoed into their smaller cavern. Kaylee sat up straight and whacked her head. "Ow!" she cried. "Are you sure it can't get in here?"

She was answered by another grunt, deep, almost musical. The way it resonated into their cavern made Kaylee think of a dropped piano.

"Follow me," Jaz whispered, crawling along their limestone beach, away from the snuffling sounds. Jaz pointed the flashlight ahead of her as she crawled into a wide but not very high tunnel, giving the shine a jerky quality.

"Where does this go?" Kaylee asked.

"I don't know," Jaz said. "If we get stuck, we can always go back."

"To the bear?"

Jaz didn't answer.

The water that had pooled in the first area was dribbling along beside them as if they were following an underground creek. In the flashlight's dim glow, Kaylee saw stalagmites and stalactites fitting together like combs, or perhaps the teeth of a whale.

She shivered and tried not to think about the massive weight of stone and rock they were crawling under.

Jaz stopped. "This is going to get tight," she said, turning to Kaylee, "but I think I see light ahead." She pointed to the narrowing tunnel ahead, the water mysteriously gone, following some other hidden tunnel deep into the earth to spring from the mountain into a river or lake.

It was tight. Kaylee would have to wiggle on her belly. "I don't see light," she said, straining for any sign that they wouldn't be heading deeper into the bowels of the earth. It was suddenly cold, and she found it hard to breathe, the dark and rock closing in on her. Swallowing, she tried to slow the beating of her heart.

"Here," Jaz said, moving to the side, covering the head of the flashlight with her hand.

Jaz's glowing red hand reminded her of a bad horror movie. She almost giggled, but remembering what was behind them, shivered instead. "At least that bear won't be able to follow."

Forcing herself forward, she wriggled past Jaz and peered into the dark. Sure enough, there was a glow. She inhaled deeply, imagining she could smell fresh air. Jaz handed her the flashlight, and Kaylee took the lead, inching forward on her elbows and belly.

She breathed a sigh of relief as the path widened and suddenly ended in a wide-open cavern. The light was coming from an opening high up in the rock—about the height of a three-story building. Kaylee's heart sank. They wouldn't be getting out that way.

"Well," Jaz said, "we can always go back."

The natural light from above cast a grayish pallor inside the cave. Kaylee gulped, spotting animal skeletons with horns still attached neatly laid out at her feet. They gleamed white, like they had been there for ages. Some time long ago, Dall's sheep must have come in through the opening to find shelter, and fallen to their deaths. She looked again at the opening above. Something must have blocked it enough that no more animals fell through.

Jaz had picked her way to the other side of the cave. "Shine that light over here," she called, peering through another opening.

Kaylee stepped carefully, not wanting to disturb any of the bones, and passed Jaz the flashlight.

There were several openings in the cavern, all of them roughly the size of the one they had just left. None of them hinted at light on the other end.

Jaz turned to Kaylee. "Which one do you want to try?"

Kaylee looked back at the tunnel they'd just come from. She didn't relish the idea of crawling back into that wet narrow space, but knew it was a safe way out if they needed it—as long as the bear had gone.

The light above them was so hopeful. She wished she had a rope.

Jaz was leaning into one tunnel. "This one goes down," she called, her voice muffled.

Kaylee shook her head. "If it goes down we could be going down forever," she said, feeling into another tunnel. "Shine that light in here, Jaz. I think this one goes up."

Jaz ducked, then disappeared inside the tunnel. "You're right," she called. "Want to try it?"

After the first few feet, the tunnel opened high enough for them to walk, as long as they bent at the waist. Before long Kaylee's back and neck were screaming in pain. She was just about to suggest a rest, when Jaz started jogging ahead.

"Light!" she called.

Just like that, they were through. Even though it was cloudy, the brightness of the day stung Kaylee's eyes. Brilliant green ferns as tall as sunflowers and bushes laden with fat blue and red berries surrounded them. She could hear the splash and tumble of water somewhere close by. Except for the horrible smell of rotten eggs, it was like a beautiful garden.

She looked about, wide-eyed. "Where are we?"

9

It was as if they'd suddenly jumped into another world —like in the *Narnia* books when those kids went into a closet and came out in a land of magic. Kaylee half expected to see a goat-boy. But instead of a lamppost in the middle of the woods, a small waterfall cascaded down the rock beside them, trickling into a stream of water, jumbling over rounded stones of white and gray and disappearing into a tangle of trees.

"Blaghh!" Kaylee said, holding her nose. "What died?"

"I know that smell," Jaz said, sniffing. "It's sulfur. I'll bet there's a hot spring near here."

Kaylee had read about a couple of hot springs near the South Nahanni River, but they weren't anywhere near Hidden Lodge.

She turned to Jaz. "How far did we crawl?"

The other girl shrugged. "I dunno. Should we check it out?"

Kaylee looked longingly at the pretty creek edged by spongy green moss and sniffed deeply, wondering where the hot spring was hidden. She liked exploring better than almost anything. She and Sausage had spent many hours in the woods at Booker Bay.

She shook her head. "We'd better get back to the lodge —we can come back later."

"Right," Jaz agreed, with her trademark nod.

"But which way?" Kaylee asked, looking up at the wall of rock they'd just climbed through and at the peaks surrounding them. Which one held Jaz's cave? She tried to remember if the tunnel they'd crawled through had been straight, or if it had twisted. They could have crawled right underneath where they were standing.

Jaz scratched her cheek, leaving a dirty smear. "We weren't in the tunnel for long. What does your compass say?"

The compass — she'd forgotten all about it! She pulled it from her pocket and held it so that they could both see. Southwest pointed to the right side of the mountain slope. "I guess we go that way," she said.

Jaz nodded. "Let's climb first. There aren't as many trees higher up. We'll be able to see better."

Kaylee waved away mosquitoes buzzing about her head and picked a path up the mountain. She was soon short of breath, but kept going.

"How long ago did you leave Uncle Jack?" Jaz asked from somewhere behind. "Do you think he's worried you got lost?"

"Nah," Kaylee said, puffing slightly. "I go hiking all the time — he knew I wouldn't get lost."

"But we are lost." Jaz pointed out.

Kaylee said nothing.

"Do you think Sausage is okay?" Jaz asked.

Kaylee climbed faster.

Finally, they came to what Kaylee figured was the other side of the slope. She checked the compass. Southwest would take them back down into a shallow valley.

"Wait up!" Jaz called, finally catching her.

"Do you recognize anything?" Kaylee asked. Her heart sank as the other girl shook her head. "The thing is, we know the lodge is southwest of Jack, and of your cave...but we don't know where we are right now. What if we came out of the mountain too far west?" She pointed toward the valley. "If we walk that way and we're too far, we could miss the lodge and keep walking forever."

"Or until we starve to death or get eaten by a wild animal."

Kaylee looked at her sharply. Some sense of humor this kid had.

"Should we climb higher?" Jaz asked, scanning the slope above them. "Maybe we'll see the Nahanni."

"We could," Kaylee said. "But all of these peaks are about the same height. We won't be able to see past any one of them." She checked the compass again. "You've spent a lot of time exploring along the South Nahanni, right?"

Jaz nodded.

"I think we should head back east until we hit the river. Maybe there you'll know where we are."

"Good," Jaz said, "Let's go."

Compass in hand, Kaylee led the way and soon picked up an animal trail. A good sign, she thought. Animals need water. This path could lead straight to the river.

Her blood tingled as it always did when she was hiking. Feeling twisted tree roots and stones through the bottoms of her hiking boots, she felt...connected. She only wished Sausage was with her — and that Jack wasn't hurt and waiting for help.

The trail led them down-slope at first, then up, and then down again. As she walked, she grasped the scratchy trunks of lodgepole pine and smooth shoots of paper birch and aspen. A mosquito bit, and she slapped her neck.

"Guess the bug juice has worn off," she said out loud.

Jaz looked at her, and Kaylee explained.

"I never go out without spraying myself," Jaz said, "especially if I'm going to be near someplace swampy."

Kaylee stopped and looked at her.

"Jaz...are there any swampy places near your cave? Just before you found me, I was getting swarmed pretty bad." She slapped her neck again. "Kind of like this."

Spotting a rocky outcrop, she broke from the path and sprinted toward it.

"Where are you going?" Jaz called.

Without answering, she stood at the rock's edge, looking from one side to the other. "Jaz, come here!" she called, reaching over the edge and uprooting a dark green, lemony smelling plant. "I know where we are!"

Jaz held Kaylee's hands as she lowered herself down the rock surface. Once she was back on the ground, Kaylee offered her shoulders to help Jaz down. They took off at a trot — first toward Jaz's cave and beyond that to the path that led back home. They ran without talking. Kaylee strained her ears listening for bear sounds, or maybe familiar barking.

At the South Nahanni they stopped to catch their breath. Once again, its beauty stunned Kaylee. Towering walls of stone rose from dark water. The river seemed to be rushing past with greater urgency than before.

"It's the rain," Jaz said, puffing, reading her mind. "It's what makes the river so dangerous. We get lots of flash floods."

"I hope Jack is okay," Kaylee said, glancing upriver.

"I'm sure he is," Jaz said, biting her lip. "Probably wet, though."

As they resumed their jog, a new worry popped into Kaylee's head. What if Sausage hadn't been able to find his way back to the lodge? The rain would have washed the scent of Jaz's footsteps away, and he would have had nothing to follow. Her stomach knotted at the thought that he might be lost in the wilderness.

Finally, they reached the lodge. Kaylee whistled, waited a long moment and whistled again. Sausage hadn't returned.

Inside the radio room, Kaylee dialed the emergency channel and listened. Nothing. The problem had to be with the emergency locator beacon, not with Jack's radio. She picked up the handheld mike and pressed the lever with her thumb. "Jack, are you there?" she called, remembering to let go of the lever in order to hear. "Jack?" she called again, frowning.

While Kaylee waited for an answer, Jaz opened the case holding the satellite phone. She gave Kaylee a thumbs-up, but she looked anxious.

"*Kaylee*?"

The call was faint, and there was plenty of static, but it was there.

"Jack! I'm here—we're here," she said, grinning. "Jaz found me on the way home. She's calling for help right now. Boy, have I got some stuff to tell you!"

"I'm sure you do…" Jack stopped speaking, but the static continued. He hadn't released the frequency. After a few moments he spoke again. *"Kaylee? Are you there?… hang on."*

She heard a banging sound, and then the radio cut out.

"Jack…are you still there?" Kaylee called.

" …sorry… sticks… sometimes… here… wet."

She grinned. Chatting on the radio was kind of like using a set of walkie-talkies, like the pink ones she had when she was little. She was suddenly swamped by a memory of hiking with her dad. They used to play a wilderness game of hide-and-seek using the walkie-talkies and a compass.

She pressed the lever again. "Yeah…I've never seen it pour like that."

A sharp burst of static, but no voice.

"Jack? Can you say that again?"

The static burst was longer this time.

"I'm not reading you, Jack."

The next burst of static was longer still, but

she could hear Jack's voice. It was faint. Jaz was talking on the satellite phone. Kaylee motioned for her to be quiet a moment.

"Just a minute," she heard Jaz say as she put her ear closer to the radio.

"... *bad*..."

Frowning, she held the mike to her mouth. "What's bad, Jack? Is something wrong?"

Another static burst, then, *"... bear!"*

She looked at Jaz in alarm. Jaz's eyes were wide. The static continued. Jack's mike button must be stuck again.

Suddenly, she heard him curse, followed by what sounded like a gunshot.

Then, nothing.

10

"Oh my gosh, Jaz—the bears!"

Jaz's face was all skewered up. "Uncle Jack..." She stared at the phone in her hand, as if she'd just remembered it. "You've got to come now!" she shouted into the receiver. She listened for a few moments and hung up, tears streaming down her cheeks.

Kaylee waited.

"A pilot that flew over a while ago called in saying he heard the emergency signal, but just for a few seconds. They already have pilots ready to go and check it out."

"That's good then, right?"

Jaz shook her head. "The weather is bad,

and they haven't been able to take off. They said they'd come as soon as they can."

"What about taking a boat?"

"You saw how fast the current is. We'd never make it through the canyon." She pounded her fist on the desk. "Stupid rain!"

In the short time she'd known her, Kaylee had thought Jaz tough, like she could handle anything. Kaylee hugged her. "It's okay," she said, through her own tears. "Jack has the flare gun. He'll be okay."

Jaz pushed herself away, wiping her eyes.

"How many bears were there?" she asked in a small voice.

Kaylee shuddered, remembering the horrible sight at the mouth of Bear Canyon. "I'm sure they didn't all find Jack."

"How many?" Jaz insisted.

"I think there were twelve...but really, Jaz, they don't travel in packs. The only reason they were all together was because of the caribou."

"I can't take that chance," she said, moving toward the door.

"Jaz, wait." Kaylee grabbed at her sleeve. "Where are you going?"

Jaz shrugged her off. "I'm going to help my uncle."

"How?" Kaylee cried. "You can't fight a bear!"

Jaz paced back and forth, her fists stuck in the pockets of her pants. "I've got to do something," she said.

Kaylee picked the radio mike back up. "Jack?" she called. There was no response. "Jack, are you there?" She called again. There wasn't even a burst of static. Either the radio was no longer working, or... Kaylee gulped. Jaz was crying again.

Kaylee leaned heavily on the counter, remembering Jack chopping wood, teasing her, waving at her from his truck. He had to be okay.

"Take the Beaver," Jaz said suddenly, breaking the silence.

Kaylee looked at her, shocked. "What?"

"You heard me."

"I can't do that, Jaz!"

"Why not? You did it before."

The idea of it settled in her gut like a stone. It was like she was back in the middle of Booker Bay, trapped by a forest fire, with the only way out, up. Except this time there was no fire. And this time, it was Jack who needed to be saved.

If it wasn't already too late.

"I don't know if I can fly a Beaver," she said weakly. "It's different from Mom's plane."

"You've got to try," Jaz pleaded. "At least come and look."

Jogging down the wooden planks of the dock, Kaylee could hear in her head the roaring freight train sound of a forest fire. Maybe this time the fire wasn't real, but she still felt like it was chasing her. She tried to block it out and remember everything Jack had told her about the Beaver.

He said it was the best airplane when there wasn't much space to land or take off. He said anything this plane could get into, it could get out of.

She desperately wanted out of this.

She slid into the pilot seat. Jaz sat in the right seat beside her.

"Well?" Jaz asked.

Kaylee ran her hands along the control panel, touching the air speed indicator, the altimeter and the compass. The starter switch was on the lower left side. The throttle was in the center and the elevator trim wheel was on the ceiling above her head.

It was different from the Cessna, but she recognized everything she needed. She swallowed. Last time she was desperate, and there didn't seem to be any other way out. Everything was different this time.

Or was it?

Jaz looked at her, silently pleading.

She and Jaz were Jack's only hope. The rescue team was held back by bad weather—likely the same weather system that had ripped through the Nahanni region earlier. Jack was stuck because of his broken leg, and he couldn't use a flare gun to hold a bear off forever … especially if the bear were determined.

Jack was like family, she thought tearfully, and he really was family to Jaz. She remembered how badly she had wanted to go back and look for her father when he had gone missing. That must be how Jaz felt.

She wasn't able to go back for her dad, but she could go after Jack.

"Okay," she said gravely. "I think I can do this."

Instead of cheering, Jaz nodded sharply and buckled her seatbelt.

"You don't have to come with me," Kaylee said. "Maybe its better if you don't."

"I'm not afraid," Jaz said. "You're doing this for me, and I trust you."

A hard lump rose in Kaylee's throat. "I'm glad you trust me, but I'm doing this for Jack. Besides, I think you'd better stay by the radio and the phone."

Jaz thought for a moment, then slipped from her seat. From the dock she called up to Kaylee. "I'll be with you on the radio all the way, Kaylee. I know you can do this."

Kaylee used the seat crank between her knees to pull herself forward and up.

As she buckled in, Jaz untied the plane, gave it a shove and pounded up the dock toward the lodge.

Kaylee increased the fuel pressure using the wobble-pump, just like Jack had shown her, started the plane and pulled away from the dock. She was suddenly grateful that her mother had insisted she study that flight manual. The need to take off facing the wind now made sense, as did how the different parts of the airplane worked with the air.

Looking at the treetops, she could tell that there was very little wind. The lake surface rippled, but there were no waves. It wouldn't matter which way she took off—or landed.

She pulled on the headset and tried the radio. "Jack? Jack, this is Kaylee, do you read?"

At first there was nothing, then, *"Kaylee this is Jaz. Just wanted you to know I'm here."*

"Thanks, Jaz."

She checked rudder movement and adjusted the flaps for take-off.

Despite the butterflies beating madly

against the walls of her stomach, she felt good. It wasn't like she hadn't done this before, and she knew way more about flying now than she had that last time.

As she increased power, the engine noise in the cockpit increased to a deafening roar, despite the headphones.

She raised the water rudders.

"Here we go," she whispered, pulling the yoke back and applying full power for take-off.

The Beaver felt like a bulldog in water as the she slooshed ahead, the nose of the aircraft rising slightly. She imagined it was like trying to run through Jell-O. As the Beaver picked up speed, its floats skimming the water, a thrill coursed through her. She was doing it! With her hands on the controls, this magnificent machine would rise through the air like a bird—a trumpeter swan.

With the aircraft at full power, Kaylee eased the yoke forward slightly. As the nose of the aircraft dropped, the tops of trees rushed toward her.

She cried out, realizing too late that she hadn't checked how much space she had for take-off.

11

As if it had suddenly turned into a cartoon version of itself, the Beaver leaped forward and into the air. Kaylee turned the wheel, banking left to clear the trees, and angled toward the center of the lake.

"Stupid, stupid, stupid!" she cried, her heart rapping hard and fast against her chest.

Her confidence had blinded her to how dangerous this really was. She climbed skyward on a steady course, terrified. She opened her mouth wide, panting, trying to draw in air—she couldn't get enough. What had she done?

The last time she had flown on her own she'd been in a plane she'd practically been brought up in. Last time her mother had been flying beside her.

There was no way to undo her take-off. She was in the middle of it now, and she was going to crash. Of course she was — she was just a kid, and she was all alone!

Tears blurred her vision. Her heart pumped so fast she was sure blood would burst through her eardrums. Gripping the yoke, her knuckles white, she climbed straight west, higher and higher.

"*Kaylee.*"

The voice on the radio startled her.

"*Kaylee,*" it called again.

Jaz. Jaz was on the radio, she remembered. Just like she said she would be.

She wasn't alone.

She took a deep breath, exhaled slowly, and loosened her grip on the yoke. "Yes ... I'm here, Jaz." She coughed and cleared her throat. "Freaked for a second, but I'm okay."

A pause. "*You sure?*"

"Yes."

And she was. As long as she didn't panic, she could do this. After all, she'd been flying since she was a baby, and she understood the mechanics of flying practically inside out.

She smiled, remembering the way her mom used to make a game of it. In the mornings, just before she went for her run, Mom would make Kaylee exercise with her. As they reached high above their heads, then forward and down to their toes, Mom would ask Kaylee to explain what they were doing.

"We're touching our toes," Kaylee would say.

"Nope. We're airplanes and this is pitch. What controls pitch?"

"The elevator," Kaylee would answer.

Her mom would then swing her arms wildly from side to side. "And what is this?" she'd ask.

Kaylee would reply, "The world's craziest mother."

"Nope, I'm an airplane and this is … "

"I know, I know. Yaw, and yaw is controlled by the rudder."

The memory was like a hug. She was okay. She could do this.

"Yaw, pitch and roll," she said out loud and turned the Beaver toward Bear Canyon.

Off her left shoulder the jagged view of mountains caught the corner of her eye. Compared to that giant silvery range, the peaks immediately surrounding the lodge were like hedgehogs to elephants. She decided to follow the river and canyon — the same way she'd gone with Jack.

"Hey, Jaz," she said into the radio mike, "your lookout above the South Nahanni looks like a foot with three big toes."

The water was still racing through the canyon, angry and dark, whitecaps slapping against sheer walls of rock. No way a boat would have made it. Within minutes she was beyond the canyon, licking her lips, scanning the area for bears. She didn't see any but knew that didn't mean anything. They could be in the trees.

As she approached the shallow lake by Jack's crashed helicopter, she reached above her head to adjust her pitch and picked up the mike.

"I'm just about ready to land," she told Jaz. "I'm going to pass over the helicopter first, then circle around."

"Do you see Jack?" the other girl asked.

If Jack were okay, he'd hear her coming. He'd probably drag himself out and wave.

She was about a hundred feet above ground when she flew over the helicopter. She strained to see inside the broken cockpit. "I can't see anything," she said, heart sinking. She flew over the shallow lake, banked left and circled back. "I'll fly over one more time and then land," she radioed. "Looks like the bears are gone."

Though she was relieved there were no honey-colored shapes humping through the trees nearby, Jack's last radio transmission echoed in her mind—his frightened cry and then the gunshot.

At the bend in the river she banked left once more and lined up to land. This time she saw movement and a flash of red flannel to the left of the downed helicopter.

Jack's shirt.

"Jaz!" she shouted. "It's Jack—he was in the trees!"

Instead of landing, she flew as low as she dared, waving. She was close enough to see Jack open his eyes wide and drop his jaw. She grinned.

Back over the floodwater, she circled left for the last time and lined up to land. If it weren't so important that she get Jack out of there, she would have enjoyed doing a few more turns. The Beaver was nicer than her mom's plane, she thought guilt-ily—way easier to fly.

She swallowed, hoping it was also way easier to land.

The water rippled, but there were still no waves—not enough wind to worry about.

The airplane dropped lower, slowing as Kaylee selected full flaps. She remembered Jack saying the Beaver could fly as slow as thirty-five miles per hour without stalling.

Out the corner of her eye, Kaylee saw silver mountains melt into greenery as she dropped lower and lower.

There were the treetops.

Lower...

She remembered not to stare at the water in front of her, instead judging her height above the water from the shoreline.

She was just about there.

The floats slapped, lifted, then slapped again.

Once she was sure the Beaver was down, she pushed in the throttle and eased back on the yoke.

She exhaled and pressed the mike button. "Jaz... this is the world's best kid pilot. I'm down and taxiing toward Jack."

"*Woo-hoo!*" Jaz's shout was so loud, Kaylee's ears buzzed.

Jack was sitting on shore, waiting, lips pulled tight, his broken leg wrapped in what must have been gauze from his medical kit and stretched straight in front of him. He must have found something to splint it with.

Kaylee stopped about twenty feet off the shore. As Jack pulled himself into the water and moved toward her, she opened the door and waved. "Hiya, Jack!" she called cheerily, as if she'd just run into him while riding her bike. Jack didn't answer until he'd reached the float and heaved himself up over the edge.

"Ahhhhhg!" he bellowed as his injured leg whacked the surface of the pontoon. He lay there, panting for a moment, then pulled himself upright. "Kaylee..." he began weakly, then clamped his jaw shut, shaking his head. He tried again. "Kaylee, I don't even know where to start."

Kaylee hung her head and quickly explained how she and Jaz had decided she would fly the Beaver to save him.

Jack put his head in his hands and left it there for a moment. When he looked up, he had tears in his eyes. "Kaylee...you're a good kid, but there's no way you should have done this. None!"

They were interrupted by a crackle from the radio.

"Kaylee? Jack?"

It was Jaz. Kaylee flicked on the mike. "I'm here Jaz," she said sheepishly. "So is Jack."

She could hear him muttering as he pulled himself up through the back cargo door, occasionally cursing and crying out in pain.

"You'll never guess who just sniffed his way in!" Jaz called.

Kaylee's heart gave a hop. "Well, I'm hoping it wasn't a bear!"

Jaz laughed. *"How'd you guess? It's the world's smallest bear, with the longest ears, and I think he wants a cookie."*

Kaylee grinned as she heard Sausage bark at his favorite word.

"Give him one then," she said. "And give him a hug for me. We'll be back in a minute."

"Move over, Kaylee," Jack grunted, pulling his leg awkwardly behind him. "I'm flying. You're sitting right seat on the way back."

"What about your leg?"

"You're going to help me." He cringed, cried out and reached to steady his leg.

Kaylee frowned. "Jack, you know I can do this. Why don't you let me fly? You can watch to make sure I don't make a mistake. Besides, you've got matching controls on the right. You can always grab them if you need to."

He wiped sweat from his forehead, his face creased with pain, and stared at her hard. "Okay, Kaylee," he said finally. "But you have to do exactly as I say."

"Of course!"

Jack buckled in, hands shaking, and glanced over her shoulder toward the shore. He frowned. "Let's get this baby turned, Kaylee—quickly!"

Kaylee turned to see a sudden rustling in the trees. She stomped hard on the rudder pedal just as a grizzly bear crashed through the woods and into the water toward them.

12

"Go, Kaylee!" Jack shouted.

The bear was huge — much bigger than the one she'd seen outside Jaz's cave. Her blood turned to ice as the bear stood on its hind legs, bellowing, gnashing its teeth. The Beaver turned as if in slow motion, and she was close enough to see the bear's black lips curl around yellowed teeth.

As soon as they were pointed the right way, she gave the Beaver full power. Jack winced as he leaned to adjust the flaps. Within seconds they were airborne. As she turned back toward Hidden Lake Lodge, the bear turned and ran toward the mountains, almost as if it were racing them home.

"What's wrong with that bear, Jack? Why did it rush out at us?"

Jack was holding his head. "I'm not sure Kaylee, but I think it might be a mama looking for her cub. She was calling something fierce, thrashing around in the bush."

"Jack, what happened while I was gone?" He sighed. "It was okay for a while, Kaylee. Wet, but okay. Then when we were talking on the radio, I heard the bear. I shot a flare through the broken window to scare it off." He shook his head. "I couldn't see anything. When I couldn't get you back on the radio, I splinted my leg and dragged myself into the woods. The bear didn't come back, and I figured I'd scared it off."

"Guess you didn't."

Jack didn't respond.

"Jack, the mike button stuck open and we heard you shoot … then we didn't hear anything. We thought … " Tears clouded her eyes. "We thought … "

Jack reached over and squeezed her hand. "Don't worry about it, honey. We're all okay now."

With Jack telling her when to turn and how high to climb, they flew between the mountains, rather than along the river. Kaylee peered at the ground, hoping to spot the cave opening and the secret hot spring she and Jaz had smelled but hadn't seen.

Jack turned on the radio and spoke into his headset. "Jaz, we're just about home, honey. Did you call search and rescue and tell them we're on our way in?"

"Uncle Jack! I'm so happy to hear you. Yeah, I called."

"Good girl," Jack said. "We're starting our approach... we'll be down in a few minutes."

Kaylee smiled. All's well that ends well, she decided, glancing toward the dock as she circled to land. Jaz had left the lodge and was waiting for them at the end of the dock. Sausage stood beside her, tongue lolling to the side of his open mouth, tail wagging. Suddenly, Sausage turned to face the woods beside the lodge. He'd stopped wagging his tail. Kaylee looked toward where he was pointed, trying to see what had caught his attention.

"Jack!" she cried.

"Stay calm, Kaylee," he soothed, "you're just about on final."

Her eyes were still glued to the shore. "Jack — a bear!"

A grizzly bear had just wandered off the mountain path onto the grounds by the lodge. It wasn't large, and it had a blonde shoulder splash. It looked like the same bear they'd seen at Jaz's cave. It must have smelled out their path. Or Sausage's.

Jaz was still waving. She hadn't noticed Sausage walking stiff legged back up the dock, and she hadn't seen the bear.

Jack leaned forward abruptly and grabbed the yoke. "I've got control," he shouted, "but I'm going to need your help. Work with me, Kaylee. Yaw right!"

Kaylee released the yoke and stomped on the rudder pedal. Jack swooped low between the dock and the bear.

As Jaz watched the plane fly by, she turned toward the bear. Her jaw dropped, and she began looking about wildly. The bear was too close...almost directly between Jaz and the lodge. She couldn't escape that way.

At the end of the clearing, Jack rose, banked right and circled for another approach. Kaylee did as she was told, hitting the rudder pedals, and adjusting the trim as Jack barked out instructions.

Sausage was now facing off with the bear, just as he had at Jaz's cave. The bear reacted differently this time, though. It was if Sausage no longer bothered him. He was standing on his hind legs, looking curiously toward the end of the dock, and Jaz, sniffing the air.

Kaylee's stomach hurt. They were so close, but other than flying back and forth, there was nothing they could do. It was as if she had been unzipped and turned inside out. Helplessly, she touched her fingers to the window glass.

Neither she nor Jack spoke as he dipped the Beaver into the clearing again. This time as they flew past, Kaylee saw the bear open his mouth and appear to yowl.

He waved a paw at them, as if he were complaining, shaking a fist.

Jaz crouched, then slipped from the end of the dock into the water.

"Jack, why didn't she take the boat? She could have made it to the boat, easy."

"If she ran the bear might chase, Kaylee. Stay focused," he said tightly and lined up for another pass.

Sausage was doing his best, growling and snapping. Kaylee clenched her fists as the bear charged Sausage, snarling, and then resumed his inspection of the dock.

"Jack ... something's happening," Kaylee said breathlessly.

She watched as the bear swung around, and stood on hind legs once more, ears pricked toward the woods. Sausage was pointed the same way, as was Jaz, half-submerged, hand grasping the end of the dock.

A milk chocolate-colored grizzly entered the clearing. It looked like it was bellowing at the smaller bear, which appeared to be bellowing back.

"Kaylee...I think that might be our mama bear from the crash site," Jack said, turning the Beaver away from the lodge.

"What are you doing?" she said, suddenly alarmed. "What about Jaz and Sausage?"

"Just wait," he said. "If that is the mother, she'll fight to protect her cub if we make another pass. Let's give nature a chance. Jaz will know what's happening."

Kaylee watched openmouthed as mother and cub reunited. The smaller bear, probably the human equivalent of a pre-teen, tackled its mother playfully, knocking her on her backside. The mother cuffed her adolescent cub about the head, and they shuffled back up the mountain path.

During the bears' reunion, Sausage had been sitting neatly in the clearing, ears perked forward, watching. Jaz had stayed hidden at the end of the dock, but she was watching too.

"Listen up, Kaylee," Jack's voice sounded warm and happy through the headset. "Why don't you take the controls again? I think you should land this baby."

"You mean it?" she asked, leaning forward. Landing was the hardest part.

"Yeah...you've proven you can handle it," he drawled, grinning. "Besides, I think this leg has had all it can take."

Jack leaned back, grimacing, and closed his eyes, but as she went through what were fast becoming familiar motions for landing, she noticed he had one eye open, watching her.

That was good, she thought. The more eyes open, the better.

13

Ignoring the smell of rotten eggs, Kaylee, with Jaz and Sausage close behind, marched past the tunnel opening and pushed through the giant ferns into what must have been a small yard, once upon a time. It was overgrown with waist-high weeds and wildflowers, rhubarb and wild rose, like a garden gone crazy. Just beyond was a small cabin, with a three-sided wood shelter to one side.

Sausage plunged through fireweed, only the white tip of his tail showing, waving like a flag, while Jaz and Kaylee moved toward the woodshed.

"Look at this big work table," Kaylee said,

wrinkling her nose, peering into the dark shelves underneath. "What do you suppose it was used for?"

"Gardening, maybe," Jaz said, shrugging.

Carefully, Kaylee reached toward the back of the bottom shelf and pulled out a short, thick glass bottle. She scratched her fingernail against the wax seal. "Or maybe mixing potions. The Nahanni has its ghosts, maybe witches too."

Jaz snorted and shook her head. "Open it."

"Should we? Maybe it's some kind of rat poison."

"No rats here." Jaz was grinning, a glint in her eye. "Lots of flowers though —maybe it's a perfume or soap. Open it!"

Kaylee looked at her friend and smiled. Jaz was the only person she knew who liked adventure as much as she did. "Okay, let's do it."

She set in on the table and scratched away the wax. "No poof of smoke," she said. "Guess it wasn't a witch's potion, after all."

"You goof!" Jaz said, laughing. "Smell it — we'll see if I'm right, and it's perfume."

Kaylee picked up the bottle, held it below her nose and sniffed. She smiled. "Nice — it's lemony. Say, maybe it's from citronella grass." She looked back at the wild garden and this time noticed a thick cluster of the same mosquito-repelling weed she'd found close to Jaz's cave.

She turned back to Jazz, watched her pull two more bottles from the shelves, scratch the top off one and sniff.

"More lemon?" Kaylee asked.

"Nope. This one's mint." She scratched the remaining wax seal. "Phew! I don't know what this is, but it STINKS! Here, smell it."

"Are you kidding? You just told me it stinks."

Jaz grinned. "Okay, maybe it doesn't stink that bad. I want to know if you recognize anything."

Kaylee held the bottle under her nose and frowned. "I smell a little mint," she said. "Maybe some lemon too ... or maybe it's just because we just had those other ones open.

There's something else in there, but I don't know what it is."

"Maybe if we keep looking we'll find more bottles," Jaz said, searching the other shelves.

Kaylee left Jaz to her latest mystery and turned toward the cabin — really not much more than a shack. It had long since gone to rot with grass growing from its roof and its door hanging crookedly, half off the hinge. The inside wasn't much bigger than a cloakroom. Smooth logs formed the walls, and a rotted red shirt hung from a hook. Everything smelled musty.

"Jaz, come see this!" she called, spotting a closed door set in one of the walls. Nearby, she heard Sausage bark.

Jaz stepped into the shack, rusty hatchet in one hand, wild onions in the other. She sniffed, taking in the dark, musty room, then nodded toward the closed door. "What's in there?"

"Maybe a secret hiding place for mysterious potion ingredients."

The door was stuck like glue—the wood moist and swollen tight in its frame. Jaz whacked at it with the hatchet she'd found, but only succeeded in breaking the head from the handle.

Kaylee rubbed her palms on her jeans. "Everything's wet and rotten. Let's look outside. Maybe there's a window into this room or whatever it is."

"Maybe it's the bathroom," Jaz said, grinning.

"Right!" Kaylee said, laughing, following her out.

Outside, the underbrush had grown tight up to both sides of the cabin. It was impossible to get through. They hiked away and fought their way back from a new angle. It was suddenly warm, and they could hear the trickle of water.

"Told you!" Jaz cried, pushing aside the final bit of vegetation. "A hot spring!"

Sausage pushed ahead, sniffing along a land bridge between the spring and a pond just beyond it. The hot spring ran right up to the edge of the cabin, where

they could see what must have been the outside face of the door they hadn't been able to open. Kaylee shook her head. "You were right, Jaz. This must have been like a big bathtub for whoever lived here."

"I bet I know who it was."

"Willy?"

Jaz laughed. "You win the …" She mouthed the word "cookie" rolling her eyes toward Sausage, who was snuffling nearby. "Look around. He did say he lived in paradise before moving to town."

"Could be," Kaylee agreed, thinking about what they'd found in the woodshed. "No sign of any prospecting tools. Maybe instead of gold, the secret he talked about was that stuff we found in bottles. Maybe he was trying to invent a super bug juice."

Suddenly there was a rustling from a marshy island set in the pond beyond the hot spring, and a great white bird rose in flight.

"The trumpeter!" Jaz cried. "This must be its nesting place!"

"So you finally found it," Kaylee said, smiling.

"Yeah, I guess so."

Kaylee sat at the edge of the hot spring, trailing her fingertips through the water. She was thinking that she had found something here too.

"Jaz, if I write you a letter, will you write back?" she asked.

The other girl plunked herself down beside Kaylee and was immediately bowled over by Sausage, who tried to crawl into her lap. "Blagh!" she struggled to avoid his dog-kisses and finally managed to settle him beside her. "Of course I will. It'll be safer than seeing this dog again. Then again, we could do that too."

"You mean holidays?"

"Why not? Once Uncle Jack gets his helicopter fixed, he'll be back to visit. I see him lots." She looked at Kaylee shyly. "Would you like to come visit?"

Kaylee smiled. "Well, if this is really Willy's place, you're going to have lots of tourists at the lodge. You could probably use a little help."

"Of course we could," Jaz said, grinning broadly. "We can never have too many pilots!"

"Oh, no!" Kaylee said, shaking her head and laughing as she shoved Jaz with her shoulder. "I plan to leave the flying to other people from now on."

Jaz shoved her back, a little harder, laughing as well. "Sure you do."

Kaylee shoved again and slipped from her perch into the steaming water, grabbing hold of Jaz as she fell. Both girls giggled and splashed each other until a deep bark caught their attention.

Kaylee laughed. "Poor Sausage … hates getting wet, but hates being left out even more."

"Is that a fact?" Jaz said. "Well then, maybe I should give him a COOKIE!"

As Sausage launched himself into the pool, joining the giggling, splashing fun, Kaylee thought Willy had been absolutely right. It might smell like rotten eggs, but this was paradise, and it had nothing to do with swans or hot springs.

"Do you like mysteries?" Jaz asked, leaning against the edge of the pool.

"Course I do."

Jaz nodded. "Me too. I think most people do ... which is why I don't think we should tell anyone about this place."

Sausage climbed back to shore, shaking the water from his coat.

"You lost me, Jaz."

"Don't you think it's more fun to try to figure out a mystery than to have someone put it on a plate in front of you?"

"I guess." She watched as Jaz broke into another of her broad, slow grins.

"Willy didn't want anyone to find his paradise. He let us find it ... but I don't think we should bring tourists here."

Kaylee watched as the great white trumpeter returned to its nest. "Maybe you're right," she said, nodding. "If too many people come here it might get wrecked."

"And then Willy would haunt us forever!" Jaz said, making her eyes go big and wiggling her fingertips in the steaming air.

Giggling, Kaylee leaned back beside Jaz,

rubbing Sausage's wet ears and watching puffs of good weather clouds sail across the heavens. She breathed deeply of wet earth and wildflowers, the fragrance mixing with and softening the sharp smell of sulfur. For the first time in a long while, she was happy to be right where she was and happy to have two best friends—even if one asked a lot of questions.

After all, if you don't ask questions, how are you going to find out what comes next?

Anita Daher has been blessed to spend time in many regions of Canada including the far north. One hot July afternoon she stumbled upon a news story about grizzly bears congregating at the mouth of a swollen river. That was all she needed. She set *Flight from Bear Canyon* in the region of the mighty and mysterious South Nahanni River in the Northwest Territories. Then, she says, it was all she could do to hang on tight and enjoy the flight of her life! Anita is the author of another book about Kaylee and Sausage, *Flight from Big Tangle*. She lives with her family in Winnipeg, Manitoba.